THIS BOOK BELONGS TO

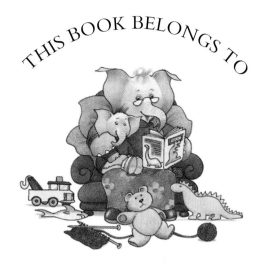

....

First published 1987 by Walker Books Ltd
87 Vauxhall Walk, London SE11 5HJ

This edition with CD published 2009

2 4 6 8 10 9 7 5 3 1

© 1987 Jill Murphy

The right of Jill Murphy to be identified as author/illustrator of this work has been asserted by her
in accordance with the Copyright, Designs and Patents Act 1988

This book has been typeset in Monotype Bembo

Printed in China

British Library Cataloguing in Publication Data:
a catalogue record for this book is available from the British Library

ISBN 978-1-4063-2087-9

www.walker.co.uk

All In One Piece

Jill Murphy

WALKER BOOKS
AND SUBSIDIARIES
LONDON • BOSTON • SYDNEY • AUCKLAND

Mr Large was getting ready for work. "Don't forget the office dinner-dance tonight, dear," he said.

"Of course I won't," said Mrs Large. "I've been thinking about it all year."

"Are children allowed at the dinner-dance?"
asked Lester.

"No," said Mrs Large. "It'll be too late
for little ones."

"What about the baby?" asked Luke.

"Granny is coming to take care of everyone,"
said Mrs Large, "so there's no need to worry."

Granny arrived at tea time. The children were already bathed and in their nightclothes. Granny gave them some painting to do while she tidied up and Mr and Mrs Large went upstairs to get ready.

Luke sneaked into the bathroom while
Mr Large was shaving.
"Will I have to shave when I grow up?"
he asked, patting foam onto his trunk.
"Go away," said Mr Large. "I don't want
you ruining my best trousers!"

The baby crept into the bedroom where
Mrs Large was putting on her make-up.
Mrs Large didn't notice until it was too late.

"Look!" said the baby. "Pretty!"

"Don't move," said Mrs Large. "Don't touch *anything*!"

Outside on the landing, things were even worse. Laura was clopping about in her mother's best shoes and beads and Lester and Luke were seeing how many toys they could cram into her new tights.

"Downstairs at *once*!" bellowed Mrs Large. "Can't I have just one night in the whole year to myself? One night when I am not covered in jam and poster-paint? One night when I can put on my new dress and walk through the front door all in one piece?"

The children went downstairs to Granny.
Mr Large followed soon after, very smart
in his best suit. At last, Mrs Large
appeared in the doorway.
"How do I look?" she asked.

"Pretty, Mummy!" gasped the children.

"What a smasher!" said Mr Large.

"You look like a film star, dear,"
  said Granny.

"Hands off!" said Mrs Large to the
  paint-smeared children.

Mr and Mrs Large got ready to leave.

"Goodbye everyone," they said. "Be good now."

The baby began to cry.

"Just go," said Granny, picking her up.

"She'll stop as soon as you've left. Have a
lovely time."

"We've escaped," said Mr Large with a smile,
closing the front door behind them.

"All in one piece," said Mrs Large, "and
not a smear of paint between us."

"Actually," said Mr Large gallantly, "you'd
look wonderful to me, even if you were
covered in paint."

Which was perfectly true ...
and just as well really!

WALKER BOOKS BY JILL MURPHY

★ THE LAST NOO-NOO

WINNER OF THE SMARTIES BOOK PRIZE, 0–5 YEARS CATEGORY • WINNER OF THE SHEFFIELD CHILDREN'S BOOK AWARD

ALL FOR ONE

★ FIVE MINUTES' PEACE

BEST BOOKS FOR BABIES AWARD

★ ALL IN ONE PIECE

HIGHLY COMMENDED FOR THE KATE GREENAWAY MEDAL

A PIECE OF CAKE • A QUIET NIGHT IN • MR LARGE IN CHARGE

THE LARGE FAMILY COLLECTION